The Hea... .. ..use

Mandy Pang

To Hannah,
Alway have fun and
lots of happy adventurs!
Mandy x HLM.

British Library Cataloguing in Publication Data: a catalogue record for this book is available from the British Library

To Collin, for your unwavering belief in me.

Gratitude

A huge and heart felt thank you to everyone who has made this possible and for those of you who have taken an interest in this book. I am overwhelmed by the support and encouragement from each and every one of you.

To Collin, thank you for being you and for gently encouraging me forward during the times where belief in myself eluded me.

A big thank you to Tom Evans, my writing mentor, and bringer of life to the idea of this book and to George.

Thank you to Harmony Kent, my editor, for your attention to detail, your kindness and technical support. Also, to Sophie Corrigan, my illustrator, for your support and beautiful illustrations.

Huge gratitude to all of my wonderful friends and personal cheerleading squad, you have all listened to my book talk with patience and encouragement.

To Amy, Doris and Evie, thank you for taking the time to read the manuscript, and for your very helpful suggestions.

Finally, a special thank you to my sisters Melissa and Sarah for your support and faith in me, and to Mum and Dad who have contributed to this book in more ways than they will ever know.

Chapter 1

In the country, on a farm, in a big red barn, there lived a family of mice. An old wooden toolbox, small but cosy, long forgotten and well hidden from the farmer and his wife, provided their home. If you were to look through its tiny windows, you would find it to be a home much like any other. Matchbox-sized beds, walls lined with family photos and paintings, a kitchen stocked with miniature plates and cutlery.

Although normally quiet and unadventurous, today this family of mice had something special to celebrate.

George opened his tenth present with reluctance, as he knew what it was before he had even torn off the shiny wrapping. He couldn't mistake its pungent smell, or the soft and waxy texture. It had to be another nugget of cheese.

George didn't want to seem ungrateful. His family had risked a lot to find these precious pieces.

'Like searching for gold,' Mum had said.

They looked so happy and expected him to feel the same.

George's heart sank to the bottom of his paws. A mouse was supposed to enjoy eating cheese. He glanced at his family, who tucked into a buffet of cheese sticks, cubed cheese, bread and cheese fondue hungrily. George stopped himself from letting out a sigh. For ten years of his life, he had eaten the same food day in, day out. The odd bit of fruit, grains of rice, and bits of cereal. And, of course, always the cheese. No matter how many different ways his mum made it, cheese tasted bland and boring. There had to be something more interesting to eat.

The heart of a mouse beats approximately 632 beats per minute. George had to make each beat count. While he blew out the candles on his Swiss Cheese birthday cake, listening to his family sing 'Happy Birthday', George wondered. The life of a mouse was meant to be small and unseen, or so his dad had always told him. But what would happen to a mouse if it stopped eating cheese? Would its heart stop beating? And what outside of this farm made his dad so afraid? Would George have a heart strong enough to find out? It seemed as if turning ten had changed something in him. George wanted more from his life, and he knew now that the time had come for something new.

Chapter 2

Upon opening his eyes from a deep sleep, George heard the raspy sounds of his family snoring. With a big stretch, he lifted off his cotton-wool duvet, and crept past his family. A peek outside showed him that the farm had transformed overnight. It looked as if someone had laid a soft white blanket over the top of the land. A festive red bow hung on the door of the farmer's house, and through the window, George could see a large Christmas tree lit up with twinkling lights. Christmas Day had arrived.

The smells coming from the house made George's whiskers stand on end. Even though it would be risky, George wanted to take a closer look. The farmer's wife had left the kitchen door open, and through it, in George snuck. Christmas carols played in the background, holly bushes framed the mantelpiece and a fire roared brightly. Unfamiliar but pleasing scents wafted around the kitchen. If he didn't think the farmer's wife would hit him over the head with her broom, he would have stood right on the countertop to get a better view.

'The turkey's nearly done,' the rosy-cheeked farmer's wife smiled.

'My favourite meal of the year.' The farmer,

who only wore his best tweed jacket on this one day of the year, winked at his little girl.

'I hope I get the penny from the Christmas pudding!' The little girl smiled at her father.

George stood completely mesmerised. He kept still and balanced himself on a tall sack of potatoes, and watched while the family ate their dinner with joy. Several times, he wanted to introduce himself and ask if he could try the turkey. Instead, he closed his eyes and imagined what it would taste like.

George didn't know how long he had been in the kitchen, but he sensed his mum would be looking for him. Just as he prepared to sneak past the family, George spotted a few pieces of food lying on the floor by the little girl's chair. As quick as a flash, George ran across the kitchen floor and grabbed a crumb. He took a quick bite and readied himself to run back to the barn. But the burst of flavour hitting his mouth stopped him in his tracks.

'You've been looking for the penny so hard, you've dropped your Christmas pudding on the floor, Jessie,' the farmer's wife said to the little girl.

'I'll pick it up.'

The little girl looked under the table, and her eyes widened in surprise when she saw there stood a little mouse with bright eyes and a long, thin tail eating her Christmas pudding. About to mention this to her parents, she stopped when the mouse smiled, thanked her for the food, and darted off through the kitchen door.

George returned home, a little disappointed to see that it looked exactly the same as when he had left it, and that there was nothing but cheese sandwiches for lunch.

Mum had noticed his absence but said nothing about it until bedtime. After the excitement of the day, George felt ready for a good night's sleep.

'You've been distracted today, George. Do you have something on your mind?'

'Mum, do you ever wonder what it would be like to eat turkey or a Brussels sprout?' George asked.

Mum looked at him, puzzled. 'Why would I, when we have cheese to eat?'

'It's just that, with all the food there is out there, maybe its time we try something different?'

Mum sighed. 'We're mice, we're supposed to eat cheese. Besides, you know how your dad feels about this sort of thing. We can't venture too far from here; it's too dangerous.'

'Have this.' Mum handed George a thimble

filled with hot liquid cheese and slid open his matchbox bed. 'It will settle you for sleep.'

George had more questions but drank it quickly. While he tried hard to remember the flavours of the Christmas pudding, George drifted off to sleep.

Chapter 3

The New Year came, and with it a new beginning. The family of mice now had company. The weather turned wet and cold, and the farmer moved the pigs and cows into the barn for shelter. Since Christmas Day, George hadn't had many opportunities to go exploring. Mum and Dad now watched him even more closely, so he kept his questions to himself.

Now, with less cheese available, the family had to share out their food carefully. Mostly, George sat around bored. The other animals paid him no interest. The cows stared at the barn walls or slept, all the while standing upright, and the pigs always seemed busy grunting and eating.

One dry, chilly day, Mum, Dad, and his older brother Alex went hunting, leaving a disappointed George to sweep the floor at home. Knowing how scarce food was at the moment, he wanted to help.

'I'm ten now; I'm not a baby anymore. I wish they would stop treating me like one,' George mumbled in a sulk.

A rustling sound came from the opposite side of the barn, and broke into his thoughts. George swivelled around in its direction and listened.

'Mmm, this is a good nut.'

A squirrel was concentrating hard, crunching through an acorn.

George didn't know what to do. He'd never met a squirrel before. Had it come to steal their food? Would it bite? He moved closer to it.

'Ahem.' George coughed quietly, hoping the squirrel would hear him.

The squirrel carried on chewing, his paws so small they were barely able to hold onto the large, shiny acorn.

George tried again, 'Hello.'

The squirrel turned mid-bite and faced George.

'Oh, hello. I didn't see you there.' The squirrel smiled.

'I'm George. Nice to meet you. Are you lost? I've never seen a squirrel around here before.'

'Well, I happened to stumble across this barn

while looking for nuts, so I thought I'd come and take a look. I'm Max.' The squirrel gave George a small wave.

'It's a nice place you have here,' the squirrel nodded to indicate his approval.

The squirrel seemed so confident and not remotely afraid.

'Weren't you frightened?' George asked. 'You couldn't have known what was inside here'.

The squirrel took another bite from his acorn and considered the question.

'Well, no, I don't think about being frightened. I'm fast, I can climb high, and I'm clever, so it would make it difficult for anyone to catch me.' The squirrel looked pleased with his answer.

George looked at the squirrel in amazement.

'Watch.' The squirrel leapt in the air, did a twirl, followed by a somersault, and landed elegantly onto the wooden frame of the barn roof.

'No one has ever caught me; I'm just too fast,' the squirrel boasted, jumping across to the opposite side of the frame.

'It takes practice and a bit of courage, but once you get the hang of it, it's a lot of fun. Weeeeee ...' The squirrel went off again, climbing higher and higher toward the top of the roof.

It appeared that the squirrel was flying, and George wished he could fly too.

Suddenly, the squirrel jumped back to the ground where he had left his acorn.

'I need to eat my nut now.'

The squirrel looked at George, then at the acorn, and back to George.

'Where are my manners? Would you like some?' The squirrel held the acorn to George, who stared at the nut.

It was buttery and solid; George's teeth struggled to bite through it. He could only eat a small amount, but liked it simply because it wasn't cheese.

The squirrel positioned himself to leave. 'I need a lot of nuts; they give me energy. I'd better go and find some more.'

'Wait, I have a question,' George called out. 'How does the nut give you energy?'

The squirrel thought George was the most inquisitive mouse he had ever met, and he had met a lot of mice on his travels.

'I don't know, young mouse. I just know that if I don't eat the nuts, I feel I can't jump as high and I get tired quickly,' the squirrel said. 'But when I have plenty of nuts, I can just ... fly.' And with that, the squirrel bounded out the door, leaving George reeling with more questions.

Chapter 4

Even though Mum thought it was too soon, George joined Dad and Alex on their weekly hunt. First, training took place in the field, every morning, after breakfast. From Alex, George learned how to strengthen his paws, mastering one-pawed press-ups, and balance walking along narrow long splints of wood. By blindfolding George and encouraging him to only use his nose and ears, Dad taught him how to smell for food without needing to search for it. Although George ached and sweated like he had never known before, he never complained. The training had made him faster, stronger, and more alert.

Dad knew all of the shortcuts, through keyholes in doors and hiding places, which the human eye could not see. Dad even took him into the farmer's house to track food, which George soon realised, took a lot of patience. The house was old and its floors were lined with creaking boards and antique furniture. Today it was silent but for the rhythmic tick-tocking of the tall mahogany grandfather clock standing in the hallway.

'The trick is never to be seen and never risk being caught,' Dad said. 'Never take more than you need; the humans will suspect, otherwise'

'I once left a piece of cheese on that chair— couldn't carry it all.' Alex nodded at a floral armchair positioned by the bay window in the living room. 'Luckily, the farmer's wife thought it was the little girl, otherwise she would have had the mouse catchers out looking for us.' Alex shivered at the thought.

Although George felt a sense of pride when he brought food home for the family, he couldn't help but feel it was wrong to take the human's food without their permission.

'They don't miss it; they've got more food than they know what to do with,' Alex said. But it still didn't sit well with George.

Still, George had never felt so free or alive than when he trained and hunted. He sensed things in his body that he had never paid attention to before. After all the running and jumping, he felt a different hunger to when he just waited for his food to be brought to him.

Just as the squirrel had said, George knew when his body needed energy, and that without it, he became clumsy and slow. He still ate cheese, but less than before, now he included more fruit, oats, and seeds into his diet.

Not until Alex commented on George no longer fitting into his t-shirts did he realise how much his muscles had grown.

'It must be all the training.' Dad winked at George.

Mum was less supportive. 'It can't be good for you, eating as little cheese as you do. Did you know cheese has protein and calcium in it, both of which are important for a mouse?' she said.

'And why do you need to eat seeds? Those are for birds, not mice!' Her voice squeaked in annoyance.

George couldn't find the right words to explain to his mum, he just knew that it was what his body needed to work better.

Chapter 5

Easter fast approached, a happy time of the year for most, but not for this family of mice. Many years ago, the farmer had hidden several Easter eggs in the barn, some in between haystacks, and one right next to the unsuspecting family's home. The mice, going about their day, like any other, were completely unprepared.

'The little girl was so excited, seeing that shiny orange Easter egg, she tripped over and nearly squashed us all in our home.' Mum recalled, shaking at the memory. 'All of my beautiful paintings ruined.'

Their belongings had been smashed into pieces, the roof and windows destroyed. It had taken a long time to make it a home they could feel safe in again.

Using shoelaces to pull up chunks of hay onto their backs, Alex, George and Dad set to work covering the outside of their house. The pigs, using the strength of their snouts, moved the wooden toolbox to the dark, shaded corner of the barn. Perhaps the little girl would be afraid of the dark and avoid looking there. It would be much colder for the mice, but safer because their house could not be seen.

To stop anyone from being able to open it from the outside, Dad had constructed a series of levers and pulleys for the roof of their home. George watched as his dad set about checking each mechanism, making sure everything worked as it should.

'We'll be leaving for your Aunt Hilda's cottage tomorrow night.' Dad turned to George. 'We will stay there until the morning after Easter. Best not take any chances.'

George hated the idea that they had to run away and hide, but said nothing.

The time at Aunt Hilda's proved uneventful. Having suffered from a broken tail following an incident with a snake, during which; 'I barely made it out alive,' Aunt Hilda would tell anyone who would listen, she had rarely left her small, cramped cottage. They read books, and ate cheese. When it came time to leave, Hilda was sad to see them go; she didn't often have company these days.

Eager to return, the family left before the sun rose, arriving early in the morning, before the farm had even begun to stir. Upon entering the barn, it became clear that the farmer, his wife, and their little girl had been here. What the mice had not expected was that the space where they had left their home, was now completely empty.

Frantically searching the whole length of the barn, until they were completely exhausted, the family of mice finally came to the realisation that their home had been taken.

Chapter 6

With the shock of having their home taken from them, and the fear of being discovered by the farmer, or even worse, mouse-catchers, Mum and Dad had made the decision to move the family to Aunt Hilda's.

'It's final, and that's all I have to say about it!'

Dad said, raising his voice sharply. All George had done was to suggest they try searching for their home around the farmland.

George took a long look at the barn, and wondered, why didn't his dad want to try? Why did they need to leave and hide away? The farm was all he had ever known, the place he had always returned to, a place of safety. But it couldn't truly be their home if they couldn't live here freely.

And so it was with heavy hearts and light suitcases, that the family of mice journeyed to Aunt Hilda's. To leave behind their family home was very upsetting, but the threat of being discovered by the humans over-ruled any sadness they had.

Aunt Hilda was thrilled to see them, and delighted in her role as hostess to the point of being completely insensitive to the family's loss.

'I have prepared beds, and washed the linen. It took me all day to re-arrange the furniture to accommodate you all,' Hilda said, looking a little put out.

Alex, took in the tiny, pokey cottage and wondered how his aunt could have needed all day to move around an armchair, a table, a display cabinet, and a bookshelf, but said nothing.

'We are so grateful to you, Hilda.' Mum set down her suitcase, avoiding eye contact with her sister, as she blinked away her tears.

'I only have this armchair to sit on.' In demonstration of it being the only object in the house that she could sit on, Hilda slowly and deliberately sank into the well-worn seat. 'I've made you each a cushion; the floor will have to do, I'm afraid.'

Not knowing what else to do, the family squatted on their thin, small cushions. The moment of awkward silence was broken by Alex, who lost his balance from the tiny piece of fabric Hilda had given him; it barely covered the one side of his bottom. He went crashing backwards right onto the antique cup and saucer display cabinet, and his paws flailed in the air.

Dad got up suddenly and headed out the door. 'I'm going to check the perimeter of the house, just in case we were followed.'

Still traumatized by the snake attack incident, Hilda felt rather alarmed by the thought of them being followed, and she didn't know whether to be more upset by that or the idea that her prized antique cups might have been damaged.

'When your mum wanted to settle in the barn, I knew it was a bad idea. I knew from the minute I agreed to it.'

Outside, Dad was pacing back and forth and muttering to himself. 'We're mice. We should always be in hiding. We aren't free to roam around like other creatures.'

George cleared his throat. 'I was thinking, Dad, that maybe we could investigate the woods nearby. Perhaps we'll find some where for our new home?'

George could see that the very thought of this panicked his dad, and his heart sank.

'We've just lost everything that took us so long to re-build. How could you even suggest that George?' his dad said. For the first time, George could see his father's disappointment in him.

'There is no safe place in the woods, or on the farm, or anywhere where we can be found by humans.'

'But, we can't just hide. We deserve a place in the world too. We belong here just as much as the other creatures do.' George's voice rose with determination. With his whole heart, he believed in what he said.

'I will not hear of this anymore, George. All this talk is utter nonsense. Don't go putting these ridiculous ideas into your mum's or brother's head; you'll put us all in danger!'

With that, Dad walked back into the cottage leaving his anger lingering in the air like a dark cloud.

Chapter 7

The days following the harsh exchange of words between George and his dad passed without event, instead they were filled with cheese. Being brought up the old fashioned way, Aunt Hilda insisted on having cheese at every mealtime. She believed that a mouse would turn into a bag of bones if not regularly fed cheese and that it was the cure for anything from a cold to a broken paw.

The small space in which they all lived together became unbearably cramped and stuffy, made worse by the intense heat of the sun that streamed through the thin windows surrounding the house.

George, now as quiet as ever and lethargic from being constantly fed nothing but cheese, had lost all hope and interest in the world outside. On his arms and legs, flab hung where his muscles had once stood proud. Even his baggy t-shirts couldn't hide his middle, which gave him the appearance of a mouse trapped inside the hole of a donut.

It was easier this way for George. It meant no risk of upsetting his mum or challenging his dad with his thoughts and ideas. George just ate cheese. At breakfast on toast, at lunch melted down into a soup, and at supper in a chunk as it came. He ate until his thoughts and ideas became a fuzzy blur that he didn't need to do anything about.

The taste of Christmas pudding, faded into a long-distant memory until George had forgotten about it altogether. He no longer remembered the surprise of something sharp or the curiosity of something sour. It ended up just like before: as if it were only cheese that ever existed.

Still, there was something comforting with all of them eating together like this. Sometimes, they would share funny stories, lifting the mood of an otherwise dull day. At other times, they would eat in silence, each lost in their own thoughts.

For Mum and Dad, these mealtimes were important. As long as they could eat what was familiar, and as long as they had their children around them, no harm could reach them. In this routine, they knew what to expect and that they were safe where they were.

And George may have been content with this life, the predictability of it, if it weren't for the day that he crossed paths with the flying squirrel again.

Chapter 8

Aunt Hilda's cottage sat at the border of the Creaking Woods, so called because of the abundance of ancient and magnificent trees, which swayed and creaked in the wind. Hilda had, over the years, through fear of a further snake attack, hidden her home at the side of a path leading into the woods, well concealed behind a border of billowing wild shrubs and hedges.

The squirrel had found a particularly large hazelnut while out exploring in a field several metres away from the woods. Not believing his luck at this find, he hadn't even considered what a struggle it would be to transport it back home. The hazelnut was so big and shiny that it slipped from the squirrel's small, tired paws and bounced away from the path. Encouraged by the gentle summer breeze, the hazelnut continued to roll toward the border that surrounded Aunt Hilda's cottage; crashing right through her hedge.

Hilda, being a creature of habit, stood out in the front garden cleaning the collection of gnomes she had acquired over the years. Originally, she had intended for the gnomes to guard her home in the event of a further snake attack, but out of loneliness, she found that they kept her company too. She was having a particularly nice conversation with Gilbert the book-reading gnome, when she heard a loud crashing sound coming from the direction of the hedges. Always on high alert, Hilda sensed danger of the reptilian variety and screamed: 'Snake, snake!!' Dropping Gilbert to the floor and abandoning him, she ran into the house and hid behind her armchair.

Out of confusion and not having enough time to process what was happening, George, Alex, Mum and Dad looked around for somewhere to hide. Due to the lack of space and furniture, they had limited success and made themselves small enough to fit into a tiny corner next to the kitchen sink. Afraid to make any noise, and keeping themselves as still as statues, they all listened.

The squirrel was a little out of breath, having

chased after the hazelnut. Following the big hole in the hedge that the rolling nut had made, the squirrel now saw that the hazelnut was resting against the wall of a tiny cottage. How odd, the squirrel thought, scratching its head. A cottage, in the middle of nowhere, and hidden from view.

Forgetting for a moment about the hazelnut, the squirrel became curious. Looking left and right for signs of the occupier, it walked through the front door, wondering what inside there was to find.

As the door slowly creaked open, Hilda found her self filled with fear and anger. She grabbed her walking stick, which she had left resting beside her armchair, and raised it above her head, ready to strike the slippery snake. George and his family watched with wide eyes, rooted to the spot, and wondered what Aunt Hilda would do next.

The squirrel entered the living room, with its bushy red tail high up in the air, and thought how pleasant it would be to meet someone new. Sensing something close by, the squirrel turned its head to the left and saw an angry, elderly mouse holding what looked like a matchstick above her head. What happened next took the squirrel completely by surprise. He felt a sharp bash on his head, followed by the sight of a group of stars twirling before him. Before he could ask the elderly mouse what had happened, the lights went out and he slumped to the floor.

Ignoring the fact that it was a squirrel and not a snake that was lying on the floor, Hilda jumped up and down, triumphant. 'You wicked snake. You thought you could fool me. Well, not this time. I was ready for you.' She steadied herself again to have another go at bashing what George and his family could clearly see was a squirrel.

'Wait! I know this squirrel; I met it in the barn a few months ago.' George ran over to the squirrel, and placed himself between it and the now wild looking Hilda.

'Don't let it fool you; it's pretending to be asleep. Although, it does look a lot fatter and hairier than the other snake.' Hilda moved closer, trying to prod the creature with her walking stick.

'It's not a snake!' George and Alex both cried.

George told them about the day he had met Max, and about how brave and strong the squirrel seemed; flying through the air.

'I say we tie it up and interrogate it. How did it know we were here? It's probably part of an organisation of cunning mice-eating snakes; they're all out to get us.' Hilda, waving her walking stick around, got all fired up again.

'How about you sit in your cosy chair, and I

make us a nice cup of tea. There's been too much excitement for one day.' Mum led Hilda to her armchair and moved her walking stick where it was out of her reach.

'Is he okay?' said George.

Alex gave the squirrel a gentle prod. The squirrel let out a big sigh and without any warning, opened its eyes and leap on to its feet. Blinking in confusion, the squirrel remembered where it was.

'How do you do? You must be the occupiers of this lovely home.' The squirrel introduced itself, ignoring the fact that one of these mice had just attacked him.

'Do you remember me? I'm George, from the barn?'

'Of course I do. The curious mouse; how nice to see you again.' In recognition of George, the squirrel grinned, baring its big white teeth.

Mum made them each a cup of tea. In the small space on the floor, they sat and listened to the squirrel tell its story of how he came to find the cottage.

'And what a coincidence that the hazelnut should lead me to the very place that you happen to now be living in, curious little mouse. Of course, they say there never are any coincidences,' the squirrel said knowingly to George.

'Are you quite sure that he didn't follow you here? Can you trust him?' Dad whispered, though not quietly enough that the others, including the squirrel, couldn't hear him.

The squirrel smiled and ignored this.

'That's what I love about being a squirrel. You never know what adventures you'll have and who you might meet along the way.'

'Your family must be expecting you, Max.' Mum, having never had a conversation with a squirrel before, felt uneasy with it being there.

'The light is beginning to fall, and I expect you will need to set off soon.'

The squirrel sniffed the air and checked the light outside, calculating his course home. 'I would say that I am precisely twenty-three minutes off course from the time of my expected return.'

'Has the snake gone?' Hilda called from her armchair.

'Yes, it's gone,' Alex said and rolled his eyes.

'Where is it that you live, exactly?' Dad asked.

'In the Creaking Woods. The tree we live in has been our family home for many years. We share it with the birds, the insects, and the caterpillars, among other things.' The squirrel prepared itself to leave and was now forming a plan in its head to get the hazelnut home.

'You mean you share your home with other

creatures? That sounds dangerous. I expect they steal your food and take your things?' Dad said suspiciously.

'We work and live around each other; it's just what we do.' The squirrel shrugged.

'There must be a lot of snakes there in those woods,' Hilda said.

'We come across them occasionally. They take what they want and then go about their way.' The squirrel realised that even though mice as a group, were curious things, they seemed to know so little of the world outside their own small one.

'The Creaking Wood is a special place to live, and the variety of food is wonderful. We have juicy berries, mushrooms that hold the flavours of the earth and, of course, lots of nuts. You're welcome to visit anytime.' The squirrel could see from their faces that the mice would never want to visit the woods. They were too afraid of what they had never known.

The light faded a fraction more, and the squirrel moved toward the door.

In his mind, George saw the past ten years of his life flash by, like flicking through the photos of a well-worn family album. He was flooded with all of the wonderful memories he had shared with his family. But he also saw how little he had experienced outside of this.

With a strange mixture of sadness and excitement, George knew that he had to leave this life and follow the squirrel into the woods.

Gathering a few things in his backpack, George turned to his family and said as gently as possible: 'I need to go with Max. I want to help him, and I want to see what's in the woods.'

Mum started to cry. 'No, it's not safe, George.'

'We discussed this. We aren't meant to do

the things that these other creatures do.' Dad's voice sounded strained. 'We're mice. We know our place. We aren't meant to have adventures or eat berries. We hide, we eat cheese, and we stay together.'

'How could you do this, after everything we've lost?' Alex looked angry, and George could see he too fought back tears.

"You can't survive out there. You're not strong enough George. You're just a little mouse,' Mum said through her sobs.

'If you leave here, you can't ever come back. I will not let you put us at risk of losing our home again, and if that means losing you, then so be it.' George could tell from the firmness of his voice, that his dad meant every word.

Standing at the door now, tears sprang from George's eyes, and a pain shot through his chest. He took a long look at the faces of the family whom he loved with all of his heart. Gathering all the strength and courage he could muster, George turned away from them to leave, closing the door softly behind him.

Chapter 9

George was as white as a sheet and appeared to be breathing sharply. Having never been involved in any serious family arguments before, Max wasn't quite sure what to do. 'Well, that was intense,' was all he could think of to say, more to himself than to George, who was now beginning to feel the weight of his decision.

'Are you sure you want to do this? To leave your family behind?' the squirrel asked George. This seemed to make George breathe even more sharply than before, which alarmed the squirrel further.

'Let's just take a slow, deep breath and we'll keep walking.' Breathing slowly seemed to help Max, too, and he knew George needed him to take charge of the situation.

'There is so much to show you. The woods are magnificent. Trust me, you won't regret it.' Both Max and George knew this to be true.

'Let's get the hazelnut home; my family will be waiting,' Max said with determination.

With a specific task to focus on, George walked with a bit more of a spring in his otherwise uncertain steps. 'We need to strap the hazelnut up with something strong, and that way we can pull it out.'

The hazelnut sat in a groove in the front of the house and did not seem to want to budge, even as Max pushed it with all his might.

Pulling out the bootlaces he had packed earlier, George quickly set about tying knots and pulleys around the hazelnut. Max watched intently; he had never thought to do this before.

'That should do it,' George said with satisfaction, giving the bootlaces a tug to check they were securely in position.

'Little mouse, you have saved me a lot of time and effort. It would have been really difficult pushing this all the way home by myself,' Max said, impressed.

'Shall we set off now?'

George tried to keep his mind on the task at hand; all the while hoping his dad might come out and say that he had changed his mind and give George his blessing. But his dad never did and as they moved through the hole in the hedge and onto the path leading into the woods, a new wave of sadness overcame him.

Without George saying a word, Max seemed to understand. 'My family will be so happy to welcome you into our home. They love meeting new people.' He smiled at George. George gave Max a nod and pulled the end of the bootstrap over his shoulder, gripping it tightly.

'I'm ready.'

The light faded more quickly now, and George felt hungry and tired. All the while Max chatted away, George thought about his family. How Aunt Hilda would be fussing over her cushions, and how his mum would be preparing the evening meal. He couldn't help but think that he could be sitting at the table with them, eating cheese and feeling comfortable. But then he remembered how stifling that familiarity had become, and how he had longed to see new things. Now, with each step he took toward the woods, he sensed the beginnings of something exciting.

'Welcome to my home,' Max said waving his hand with a flourish over the grandest oak tree George had ever seen. The tree must have been about eighty feet tall and appeared to disappear up into the sky. George touched the nearest part of the tree where he stood, and felt the grounded strength of its trunk, from which many branches filled with vibrant green leaves sprung.

'Evening, Max,' a snail wearing a bright red bowler hat said while he shuffled past them.

'Looks like... you've... made a good...catch... today,' the snail said, drawing out each word in a long, heavy manner.

'Jeffrey, let me introduce you to George. He's new to the neighbourhood.'

George felt unsure how the react to the snail. Why was it wearing a hat?

The snail, though slow in pace and speech, was very observant. 'You...must be...wondering... about the...hat?' it asked George.

Before George could think of something to say, the snail answered, sounding each word carefully, 'My shell...is completely...full, and...I needed more...storage space, and the...hat seemed like...the logical answer. You'd be... amazed...at how much...stuff I can...keep...in it.'

'Well, it's nice to meet you, and it is a great hat.' Now that the snail had explained, the hat seemed to make sense.

Max entered a door at the base of the tree trunk and signalled for George to follow, then turned to the snail and said goodbye.

They moved into a small, narrow hallway, filled with scarves, gloves, and bags. Chatter and laughter came from the room ahead, which was bathed in a warm glow of welcoming light and unusual smells.

'Dad's back!' a little squirrel, identical in looks to Max said, and then leapt up to greet his dad. Three other young squirrels followed, and Max gave them each a big hug.

'Who is this, Dad?'

'Why are you so late?'

'Oooh, a hazelnut, it's so big!'

'Can we make chocolate hazelnut spread, Dad? It's my favourite, pleaassseeee.'

The voices all spoke at once, and George couldn't tell which question came from which squirrel.

'Now, give your father a chance to settle in, he's only just come back,' a female squirrel said. She wore an apron, which she wiped her hands on before giving Max a big hug and greeting George with a friendly smile. Grouping the little squirrels together, she then led them back into the living room.

Max followed them into the room and introduced his family. 'George, this is my wife, Jacqueline. I met her on my travels in Paris.' George didn't know why it surprised him that Max had been somewhere as far away as France;

he was the most adventurous creature he had
ever met.

'These are our little ones: Hazel, Acorn,
Almond and Chestnut.' The little squirrels
squealed with laughter.

'That's not our names, Dad; you're being silly
again.' The older of the little squirrels giggled.
'I'm Pippy; this is my little sister, Lotty, and my
little brother, Manny.'

'And I'm Francois. I was born in Paris,' the
older male squirrel said proudly.

'Well, nice to meet you all, and thank you so
much for welcoming me into your home.'

And George did feel welcome. Jacqueline
made sure his bowl was never left empty, and
kept it filled with lots of delicious food. They
started with a warming onion soup, followed by
a dish of earthy, meaty mushrooms covered in
a rich, creamy béchamel sauce. Filling himself

up with these wonderful new flavours, George didn't think he could manage another bite.

'You have to have dessert. It's the best bit.' With all of his soup and mushrooms finished, Manny held his spoon expectantly, ready for his dessert.

'I made you your favourite, raspberry and mint sorbet.' Jacqueline winked at Manny, setting down the brightly coloured dessert on the table. Even looking at it made George happy, and taking the first grainy spoonful, the sorbet melted into an explosion of flavour. Having only tasted the mellowness of cheese for most his of life, the sharp sweetness of the raspberries and the cool mint took him by surprise.

'Thank you, Jacqueline,' he said. 'It was all wonderful.' George felt full but satisfied. Even though he felt the heaviness of the day, he somehow felt more energised from the food he had eaten.

It was a good job too; Pippy, Manny, Francois, and Lotty were curious about their new visitor and had many questions for him.

'Where's the rest of your family then?' Lotty asked.

'That is a story for another day, little ones. Off to bed now,' Max said and led them all off to their bedrooms.

Max pointed to a door on the left of the living room and said to George, 'Have a good night's sleep. I have lots to show you tomorrow.'

After the house had become quiet and still, George lay in his warm, cosy bed and collected his thoughts. Had he made a mistake leaving his family behind? Would he ever see them again? The dark night sky looked clear but for the littering of stars sprinkled across it. From the window, George looked up and imagined that his family were at that very moment looking at the same stars. He wished them each goodnight, and with a dull longing in his heart, he closed his eyes and drifted off to sleep.

'It's breakfast time!' George awoke to four bright, little faces looking at him. Having eaten so well last night, George was surprised to find his stomach grumbling with hunger, and he let the excited little squirrels lead him to breakfast.

'Good morning, George. Take a seat and help yourself to anything you like.' Max, who was wearing an apron and a chef's hat, waved a spatula over the table. 'I'm just about to start on the honey and lavender pancakes.'

George copied Francois, who poured a mix of nuts, seeds, oats, and dried fruit into a bowl, and reached for his spoon and took a bite.

'Mmm, yummy,' Lotty said with a big smile on her face.

'This does taste good.' George felt pleasantly surprised and enjoyed the crunch of the oats and nuts and soft pieces of dried fruit.

'We love our food in this house; it keeps us all happy and healthy,' Jacqueline said, proudly.

On a few occasions, George had searched with difficulty for cheese and had heard his dad and Alex complain how hard it was to come by. He couldn't understand how the squirrels were able to find so much to eat.

'Do you take the food from the other animals and insects?' Surely that could be the only explanation, George thought to himself.

'No, we never take what belongs to another. Here, in this tree, each animal, insect, and plant has something to offer to the other. And that way, we never go without and we always have something different.'

Seeing how confusing this was to George, Max went on to explain, 'So, if I'm in need of some honey for my pancakes ...'

'They're really good, Dad,' Manny said through a big mouthful of pancake.

'Thank you, but you really shouldn't talk with your mouth full.' Max smiled and continued, 'As I was saying, if I needed honey for my pancakes, the bees would provide me with some, and in return, I would give them some lavender, which I pick from the woods for them to eat.'

George nodded in understanding.

'Here, we each work to our strengths. We squirrels are good at gathering nuts, small plants, and flowers, and sometimes when we have too much, we give some to the creatures who can make use of them.'

George and his family had always relied on taking food from humans, and George looked at the squirrels in wonder. He saw how much better their way worked.

After plates had been cleared and tummies were full, Max said goodbye to his family, as they left for school.

'Come, let me introduce you to some of the others.'

The woodpecker was busy chipping away at a complex bit of carving when they came across him. He stopped to take a break and looked startled to find the mouse and squirrel resting next to him, watching.

'OH, DO EXCUSE ME, I DIDN'T HEAR YOU,' the woodpecker, whose ears had become damaged from years of chipping, was talking a lot louder than necessary.

It held its beak out to George in way of a

greeting, and asked him, 'WHAT BRINGS A YOUNG MOUSE LIKE YOU TO THESE PARTS?'

Nervous, George replied, 'I guess I wanted to see what was in the Creaking Wood.'

'AH, WELL YOU'RE IN FOR A TREAT. IT'S A NICE NEIGHBOURHOOD AROUND HERE.'

Raising his voice even more loudly, the woodpecker said, 'JUST DON'T STRAY TOO FAR INTO THE MIDDLE OF THE WOODS. THEY SAY THERE'S A BEAR THAT LIVES THERE, AND WHEN DISTURBED, HE WILL HUNT YOU DOWN AND EAT YOU. THEY'LL EAT ANYTHING, YOU KNOW.' The woodpecker nodded at George knowingly.

Seeing how frightened George looked at the prospect of being eaten by a bear, Max said his goodbyes to the woodpecker and moved further up and along the tree.

George followed Max, who easily found his way around the never ending twists and turns of branches and leaves. George felt clumsy and a bit queasy at the thought of how far up they had climbed. He kept his eyes on Max, now in his element, leaping from branch to branch and running up the trunk as if he were on solid ground. They came to a side of the tree facing the stream. George stopped to catch his breath, and the beauty of the sparkling light from the sun dancing on the water startled him. Lost in thought and wishing his family were with him now to share this, he felt a gentle fluttering on his shoulder.

'It's a magical sight, isn't it?' a tiny voice spoke from the direction of the fluttering on his shoulder.

'You're right, Matilda, it is,' Max said.

Still not knowing what or who the voice was, George turned around to find a brightly coloured winged insect hovering around him.

The butterfly, though a large one by butterfly standards, could not have been any bigger than an acorn. George stared at it, mesmerised. George took in its wings, and could see its purple patches of colour, blended with splashes of pink, white, and black, and all perfect, as if they had been painted on.

'A wood mouse; we haven't seen one of those in these parts for a long time.' The butterfly now hovered right above George's head as if it were inspecting him.

'Erm, well, I come from a farm. This is my first time in the woods,' George said almost apologetically and in a quiet voice, not wanting to waft away the delicate butterfly by accident.

'Well, they say these woods will test the very heart of any creature that lives here. I wonder how a heart as tiny as yours will fair,' the butterfly said.

'All in good time,' Max said smiling at George, as George panicked at the thought of having to go through some sort of test.

'Enjoy the sunshine.' And with that, the butterfly floated up toward the sun and disappeared out of sight.

'What did the butterfly mean about my heart being tested? And why does everyone seem so surprised that I'm here?' George asked Max.

'That's something we can discuss later,' said Max mysteriously. 'I've just spotted some acorns. How are you at somersaulting?'

As it turned out, George was absolutely terrible at somersaulting. His first three attempts resulted in him crashing heavily against some branches, where he knocked a few birds out of their nesting spots, much to their annoyance.

On this forth attempt, he managed a three-quarter somersault, only to land on his back, nearly squashing a family of ladybirds. It frustrated George to see Max move around with such speed and skill, and not be able to do the same himself. 'Keep practicing; you'll pick it up, you'll see.' Max reached out a paw to help George upright. 'Now, let's try again'.

Chapter 10

Everyday, George watched and listened. He practiced and worked hard, learning from Max, how to move and navigate his way around the oak tree and the creatures that lived in it, who—with each day, had started to feel like family.

Much to his surprise, George discovered he had skills that Max did not. George had a heightened sense of smell, which proved useful for avoiding rancid nuts and fruit. Being able to fit into smaller holes and burrows, George often found seeds and nuts in the most unexpected places.

Max taught him how to match footprints to different animals—a useful skill for any creature living in the woods if they didn't want to be eaten by a fox or, worse still, the bear that lived in the middle of the woods. Although these scary animals were a constant threat to the community, he was too busy hunting for food, learning to cook with Jacqueline, and meeting other creatures to think too much about it.

Everyday, he discovered something new. He loved the sound of a bee buzzing past him and the rippling of water flowing along the stream. The flowers and insects appeared to be works of art in themselves; George had never seen such colour and beauty in all of his life. The air was clean, fresh, and deeply soothing to his lungs. It felt as if his body and mind had awoken from a deep sleep, and he even lost the wobbly bit around his stomach.

His heart, which had broken on the day he left his family behind, had started to mend, but little did George know that as the days drew closer to his eleventh birthday, he would soon have to put it to the test once again.

Waking up to a cold chill in the air, George wrapped his woollen blanket more tightly around his shoulders, and looked out the window to find that the frost had crept in overnight. The whole of the tree was covered and the ground below had become one large thin sheet of ice. How magical it looked, the land frozen, as if time had stopped. Careful not to wake the family of squirrels, who each lay in a heavy slumber, George gathered his things and left the house without making a sound.

George glanced over the list of ingredients he needed to hunt for, and cast his mind to the upcoming party. Tomorrow, he would turn eleven; how old that sounded to him. It was all the entire community talked about. They loved a party, and each creature had offered their help in some way or other. His heart sank when he thought back to his last birthday. He must have appeared so ungrateful. His family had gifted him all so much cheese, and he hadn't wanted any of it. He missed his family, and the thought of celebrating his birthday without them caused George a great deal of pain. But he had made his choice, even when his dad had made it clear that it wasn't a choice at all.

George pushed these thoughts aside and

focused on the list again: wild mushrooms, Elderberries, and Sorrel. He would need to go deep into the woods to locate these. George took the path leading directly into the centre of the woods, and felt the sharp stab of the icy ground when it broke gently under the light steps of his paws. He was glad he had his hat with him, it was one he had bought when Jeffery the snail had taken him to a little hat shop owned by a silkworm. The bright yellow hat felt soft, and much warmer than one might expect from material so fine and delicate.

The sun now rose lazily and peeked out above the land, where it brought light to the flowers, plants, and trees, who all turned their heads to greet it. The woods came alive as the other creatures moved to the rhythms of a new day. Quickly, George found the berries, which hung in large clusters high up in the bushes. The sweet scent of these berries was easy to track. George, resisting the temptation to eat them all there and then, wrapped them carefully with some cloth and stored them in his rucksack.

The wild mushrooms proved more difficult to find. Max, wanting to eat something to remind him of Paris, had asked George to find him a particular type—some Chanterelle mushrooms, which Max planned to fry in butter and wild herbs. Being popular with the humans, George had been told that they were quite scarce now, and George now found this to be true.

Going deeper still into the woods, George crouched down with his nose to the ground. Max had described the mushrooms as having a fruity smell, and George narrowed in for this scent. Perhaps they lay well hidden among rocks or underneath bracken. After he had covered several lengths of foliage and ground, George had failed to locate any. Perhaps the frost had covered up the scent of the mushrooms. Stretching up from the hunched position he had been in, George realised he had gone much further into the woods than he had meant to.

The path was no longer visible. The trees here stood almost bare—their leaves separated from their branches and long fallen to the ground. These trees grew more closely together here, their gnarled branches twisted around each other, forming a roof through which very little light could break between. George couldn't recognise the plants or the wildlife, very little in the way of flowers or birds lived here. He felt the thud of his heart as it beat heavy and fast, and a wave of anxiety fell over him. He was completely lost.

George narrowed his eyes to the ground, searching desperately for signs of his paw prints. It was no use, though; the light was too dim, and the ice on the ground had melted, taking away the means to guide him home. George slumped to the ground in defeat and allowed his panic to set in. What had he been thinking, straying so far into the woods?

To keep his mind off the unfamiliar creaks and groans of the scary looking trees, which surrounded him, George took out the piece of bread and cherry jam Jacqueline had packed for him the night before. The simple, familiar act of eating, provided some comfort, and George tried to gulp down the fear which had become stuck in his throat and chest. Perhaps if he waited a while, the sun would come up enough for him to see better. Little did George know, only a few feet away, lay a very grumpy bear, whose sore tooth had forced it to awake early from its hibernation.

Chapter 11

The bear was tired, in pain, and in a very bad mood. Since the start of his hibernation, he had not slept well. Through the summer months, the bear had gorged on berries, trying to store as much food in his body as possible in preparation for the winter. This had been a mistake. The seeds from the berries had become trapped in the cavity of his back tooth, and this caused him unbearable pain. The throbbing in his tooth demanded his attention, and he awoke angrily. His stomach, registering that he hadn't had food for many weeks now, growled in hunger.

The bear lay on his side, stared into the darkness of his cave, and thought about what he should do next. He soon came to the conclusion that he needed to hunt, and although he preferred to eat plants and berries, the pain from the tooth told him this would not be a good option. He needed to hunt for meat. The bear had lived a solitary life. Being around other animals did not appeal to him at all and made him feel even grumpier.

With a loud, wild growl, the bear shook off the layer of dust which had gathered on his thick shaggy hair, and bounded out of his cave, creating a ripple on the ground, which could be felt for miles around.

The floor on which George sat shook and trembled. Immediately, he knew he was in danger. His whiskers stood on their ends and his ears raised high in anticipation of what lay ahead. George felt sure his heart would escape out of his chest, and he hoped the loud thud of its beat would not give away his location to, what he was now sure, was a bear.

Searching frantically for somewhere to hide, George crouched low to the ground and lay underneath a pile of rotting leaves, hoping the awful smell would mask his scent. Having been warned that bears are extremely sensitive to sound, George tried desperately to slow down his breathing. The bear came tearing through the trees by which George lay, and he felt sure he would be caught in a matter of moments.

The bear pushed himself upright with his paws and stood tall on his short hind legs. George trembled at the sight of its sharp claws. The bear stood still, breathing steadily. He scanned the woods for a sound, smell, or sight, which would lead him to some food. The very thought of moving from cover made George sick, but if he were to make it out alive, he would have to make a run for it.

Suddenly, a sharp noise cracked through the woods, followed by the sound of human voices. The bear turned his head in the direction of the voices, and George seized his opportunity. With the full flow of blood pumping from his heart, and gathering all of his strength into his back legs, George ran in the opposite direction.

The bear, realising that the humans had seen him, and were now in pursuit, also turned in the opposite direction to run. But the muscles in his limbs had weakened, and the lack of food had left him dizzy. His front paws lost their grip on the muddy, damp ground and he slipped clumsily. Bearing the full weight of his large body, the bear had injured his left paw.

Soon, the two humans reached the ground where the bear now lay helpless and trapped. Pointing guns at the animal, and with little regard for the wellbeing of the bear, they cast a net around it so tightly that it couldn't move an inch.

'There's no way the two of us are going to get this beast back to the truck.' The tall, skinny man had a thin moustache, and cold eyes which registered the razorblade-like sharpness of the bear's teeth.

'Fine, let's go back and get some more men. This grizzly isn't going anywhere with an injured paw.' The older man grinned cruelly at the bear.

George stopped suddenly at the wild cries coming from behind him. The bear had been captured and sounded like it was in deep pain.

George was desperate to keep running, and to be in the warmth of the squirrel family home, eating a nice plate of food that Jacqueline had promised would be waiting for him upon his return. He didn't want to be here, in these horrible woods, contemplating the rescue of a bear who would likely eat him as soon as it was able. But deep in his heart, he knew he would have to risk his life trying, he couldn't bear the thought of what the humans had in store for the poor creature.

No doubt, for this bear, this had turned out to be the worst day of his life. All he had wanted was to find some food and to get back into hibernation. The net dug into his flesh; he had probably broken his paw, and he was absolutely starving. The toothache seemed like a tap on the shoulder compared to the situation he found himself in now. So it was a huge surprise to the bear when a little mouse, carrying a rucksack, appeared before him.

George scanned the net cast around the bear's body, and spoke in a voice he hoped wouldn't betray how frightened he felt, 'I've come to help. We'll have to move quickly.' 'Oh, and please don't eat me,' George added quickly.

The bear, although he couldn't help but salivate at the thought of eating the tiny creature standing before him, kept himself very still while the mouse worked his way around the net.

George took swift bites through the rope, concentrating on the areas around the bear's head and right paw, allowing the bear to be free enough to claw and bite his way out of the net.

Darkness had begun to fall around the centre of the woods, and having used what little energy he had left to free himself, the bear found that he could hardly stand, much less crawl back to his cave.

George hesitated around the large creature, watching it carefully for any sudden movements and any signs of its sharp white teeth.

The men would return soon in greater numbers.

The bear said, 'You must help me get back to my cave; we'll be safe there.'

George had no choice. He had no way of finding his way back now, and he couldn't leave the bear to be recaptured again. He nodded. 'All right, which way?'

The cave was dark, smelly and littered with rotten berries and the bones of small animals. 'You'll find matches and candles by the entrance,' the bear said. Completely spent, the bear collapsed into a heap, wincing in pain from his injured paw.

Not wanting to be alone in the dark with an animal that was at least a hundred times bigger than himself, George got to work quickly. He found the matches and lit the candles, placing them at the far end of the cave. The bear hardly moved and took slow, shallow breaths. From his rucksack, George took out a pouch of water, the wild mushrooms and the last slice of bread. Not having the energy to thank this kind, brave mouse first, the bear gulped down the water, quickly ate the food, and promptly fell into a deep sleep.

A steady drip of water falling from the ceiling of the cave tapped the bear on his head and he knew he couldn't hibernate here. He awoke to find daylight streaming through the cave. Looking around, the bear noticed several odd things. Firstly, his left paw had been bandaged with yellow silk thread, supported by a plank of tree bark; secondly, his cave now looked clean and tidy, and thirdly, a tiny mouse lay curled up fast asleep behind a barrier of animal bones.

The bear made a gruff coughing sound and hoped that the mouse would wake up soon and leave. Dizzy with hunger, he didn't know how long he could stop himself from eating it.

George had intended on only napping for an hour or two so he could keep an eye on the bear, but finding comfort from the light of the candles and feeling safer behind a wall of animal bones, he had fallen asleep as heavily as the bear had. Feeling something large looming over him woke George with a start, and he jumped up from the cold, hard floor of the cave.

'Didn't mean to scare you,' the bear spoke as gently as possible, so as not to scare the mouse. He had heard their hearts were small and weak, and he didn't want this one to suffer a heart attack after all it had done for him.

'Oh, that's quite all right,' George said, looking for his escape route. The bear, which had appeared less frightening last night, now appeared to be all teeth, claws, and chest.

The mouse took a deep breath filling himself with courage, and asked the bear, 'How's the paw?'

'Better.' The bear held up his bandaged paw to show George.

'Why did you help me last night?' The bear had meant to thank George, but having so little contact with other animals had made him less polite than he had realised.

Shaking a little, George thought about his answer for a moment. 'I just knew it was the right thing to do, regardless of the consequences.'

The answer surprised the bear, and he let out a heavy sigh. 'I know what they say about me. That I'm a monster and all I do is smash and kill my way around the woods. But it's not true. I keep myself to myself because I like it that way. But when I'm attacked, I defend myself.' The bear growled at the thought of this.

'So I know that it takes a brave creature indeed to help me in the way you have.'

George felt relieved to see that the bear's ferociousness had softened when he said this. He asked, 'So you don't eat other animals then?'

'Well, I normally eat plants and berries, but I have this awful toothache, so I thought meat would be better for me,' the bear said.

George's heart dropped to his knees. Did the bear mean for him to be the meat?

Seeing the fear come over George at what he had said, the bear explained quickly, 'Don't worry. Although I'm sure you would taste fantastic, I can't harm a creature who has shown me the kindness you have.'

Although the bear sounded sincere, George thought that the growling from its stomach betrayed what it really thought. In an extra-squeaky voice, he said, 'I'll need to get going soon, but before I do, how about I make us some breakfast?'

While the bear sat eating a delicious herbed omelette, it thought how funny it would have looked to anyone wandering by: an enormous bear happily sitting next to this tiny mouse that possessed the biggest heart of any creature he had ever met.

Later, Max looked at George in astonishment. 'What do you mean you gave them all to the bear?' Max didn't know whether to be mad at George for returning without any of the mushrooms he had been looking forward to, or be more frightened at the thought of a bear being so close by.

'The bear was injured and hungry, and it was all I had. You understand, don't you?'

'So you finally found what your heart was truly capable of.' Max forgot his disappointment about the mushrooms and smiled broadly at George. 'From the first day we met, I knew yours would turn out to be kind and brave. Come on, we've got a birthday to celebrate!'

And what a celebration it was. Even before they had reached the magnificent oak tree, George could hear the music and laughter. At the centre of the party, a band had formed, made up of the woodpecker on the drums, Francois with his saxophone, and a choir of singing crickets.

The glow worms, who were normally very shy, swayed from side to side to the music, lighting up the forest floor with their bluey-green glow. George felt overjoyed. They had all gathered here in their best outfits to celebrate his special day. Even Jeffrey, in a bright blue top hat had made an effort, and stopped to wish George a Happy Birthday.

A long table had been filled with food. Cheese sticks, crisps, and smoked cheese and crackers, platters stacked high with wild garlic and goats cheese parcels, tomato and basil salad, and chestnut and sage spaghetti. The desserts looked so delicious and beautiful: hazelnut and wild berry meringues as big as balloons, perfect scoops of honey and ginger ice cream, and a mountain of crimson cranberry jelly, which appeared to be wibbling and wobbling in tune with the music.

'Do you like the birthday cake we made you?' The little squirrels surrounded George and jumped up and down, squealing with excitement.

'Sorry about the messy icing, but they insisted

on making your cake themselves,' Jacqueline chuckled, picking icing from Pippy's hair.

'It's chestnut, ricotta, and strawberry flavour! Hurry up and cut it so we can have some.' Manny, who had been hovering over the cake all day, took a fork from his pocket, ready for his slice.

The mouse shaped cake did indeed look quite lopsided, but it was the best birthday cake anyone had ever made him.

'Thank you,' George said simply, hugging Jacqueline and the little squirrels.

'A party isn't a party without cheese.' Turning to the direction of the voice that he hadn't heard for so long, yet one he could recognise anywhere, George, blinked in confusion. He took in the unexpected sight of his family.

'We couldn't miss your special day,' Mum said, as she blinked back her tears.

Dabbing away a tear with a handkerchief he

had kept in his jacket pocket, and then handing it to Mum, Dad looked up at George. 'I am very sorry for the way I spoke to you, George. It's all I have thought about since the day you left. You didn't let my fears stop you from following your heart. I am so proud of you.' Completely lost for words, George hugged his dad tightly. Alex and Mum joined in for a hug too and George thought his heart might burst with happiness.

Patting George on the shoulder, Aunt Hilda said simply: 'We showed them evil snakes!' then wandered off towards the table of food.

As his friends and family mingled and danced, George took a moment to break away from the party. He sat by the grand oak tree, and looked up, just in time to see a bright star shoot across the black night sky.

'They say wishing upon a shooting star makes the wish come true.' George looked down towards the gentle voice, and smiled at Matilda the butterfly, as she glided past him.

It was then that George realised, he didn't need to make a wish. He was a mouse who now had everything, all the things he was always told he could never have. By following his truth and facing his fears, George had finally discovered just how big the heart of a mouse could really be.

About the Author

Mandy Pang has loved reading books since she was a child.

Although Art and English Literature were her favourite subjects at school, her studies took her down the path of Psychology and Dietetics. Alongside her interests in writing, photography and graphic design, Mandy is currently working in a hospital as a Dietitian, in Lancashire, where she lives.

Several years ago, she decided it was time to start writing down the stories swimming around in her head. The Heart of a Mouse is the first of her children's books.

About the Illustrator

Sophie Corrigan is a freelance illustrator specializing in children's books. She is currently studying for her Masters Degree in Children's Book Illustration at the University of Central Lancashire. Her work is mainly based around animals and nature, and she often adds an element of humour and quirkiness to her characters.

Printed in Great Britain
by Amazon